The Death of Murat Idrissi

Tommy Wieringa was born in 1967 and grew up partly in the Netherlands, and partly in the tropics. He began his writing career with travel stories and journalism, and is the author of four other novels. His fiction has been shortlisted for the International IMPAC Dublin Literary Award and the Oxford/Weidenfeld Prize, and has won Holland's Libris Literature Prize.

TOMMY WIERINGA

The Death of Murat Idrissi

Translated from the Dutch
by Sam Garrett

SCRIBE
Melbourne • London

Scribe Publications
2 John St, Clerkenwell, London, WC1N 2ES, United Kingdom
18–20 Edward St, Brunswick, Victoria 3056, Australia

Originally published as *De dood van Murat Idrissi*
in Dutch by Hollands Diep in 2017

First published in English by Scribe in 2019
This edition published 2019

Text copyright © Tommy Wieringa 2017
Translation copyright © Sam Garrett 2019

Extract from T.S. Eliot's *The Waste Land* on p. 4 reprinted here
with permission of Faber and Faber Ltd

Every effort has been made to acknowledge and contact the copyright holders for
permission to reproduce material contained in this book. Any copyright holders who
have been inadvertently omitted from the acknowledgements and credits should
contact the publisher so that omissions may be rectified in subsequent editions.

Printed and bound in the UK by CPI Group (UK) Ltd, Croydon CR0 4YY

Cover design by Jenny Grigg

Scribe Publications is committed to the sustainable use of natural resources
and the use of paper products made responsibly from those resources.

9781911344896 (UK edition)
9781925713305 (Australian edition)
9781925693331 (ebook)

Catalogue records for this book are available from the
National Library of Australia and the British Library.

scribepublications.co.uk
scribepublications.com.au

For Channa

Song of Solomon 1: 15–17

So It Begins

In the deepness of time. The calm breathing of millions of years. An inland sea falls dry, evaporates beneath the blazing sun; the basin becomes a wasteland of salt. *Sol Invictus*. The searing heat of the deep desert — rain evaporates before it hits the ground, a fine mineral spray settles on the earth's surface.

And then, at the end of that silent, motionless epoch — there is no one to witness the wonder of the continent's tectonic fracture — a breach opens between the Atlantic Ocean and what will become the Mediterranean Sea. Foaming and churning, the water breaks through the rift and descends on the saline desert; the waters rise a few metres each day.

First, the basin fills from Gibraltar to Sicily; then comes the eastern part, to the coasts of Turkey and the

Levant. *Mare Nostrum. Yam Gadol. Akdeniz.* Cragged mountaintops stick out like islands.

The crack between the Eurasian and African plates is but a scratch in the earth's crust; still it divides the continents resolutely. Here is here and there is there.

From the flank of her mountain, the Neanderthal woman whose bones will be found one day in a cave on the Rock of Gibraltar can see the mountain on the far side of the strait, Jebel Musa, shimmering in the light. Does she see signs of human life there? Pillars of smoke on the horizon? Does she have *thoughts* about the other?

The life there does not impinge on hers. Too far away.

Sixty kilometres long is the Strait of Gibraltar, at its narrowest only fourteen wide; there is a powerful current. Dreaded by sailors. Sandbanks, headlands, reefs, the treacherous Boreas. The fog that drops in suddenly, obscuring the far shore.

Rising up on both sides, the Pillars of Hercules: the Rock of Gibraltar in Europe and Jebel Musa in Africa. Marking the end of the world. So far, and no further. He who ventures past this point becomes lost in the mist beyond.

More water dissipates from the Mediterranean than the Nile, the Rhone, and other rivers can replenish; there is a huge influx from the Atlantic. At the same time, through the Strait an undercurrent of heavy, saline water slips back into the ocean.

Current, counter-current, wind, contrary wind; it rages between the mountains on both sides of the Strait. All you can do is brace yourself and pray to be saved.

Six thousand years ago, not far from Gibraltar, on a rock close to Jimena de la Frontera, someone drew an ochre-coloured ship; it has a sail, oars are sticking out from the gunwale. It is the world's oldest depiction of a sailing ship. Perhaps it is a ship used for fishing along the coast, perhaps for commerce between Europe and Africa — though no evidence exists for such early traffic between the continents.

For a Bronze Age vessel, the route from Spain to Morocco would have been a risky enough enterprise; a venture from the Mediterranean to the Atlantic would have meant its certain demise. The end of the world is the death by drowning that awaits you there.

Still, someone was the first to get past the Strait of Gibraltar. Steely waves below him, their cold gleam.

The sea of monsters and sunken empires. The ocean without an other side.

The captain's name has been lost to time. A Cretan, blown by the storm? Or else a Phoenician, shipwrecked in the mist? *A current under sea picked his bones in whispers ...*

Galley men at their oars, the Phoenicians row past the Pillars, against the Atlantic current. They establish the trading post of Mogador on the African coast and the colony of Gadir at the mouth of the Spanish Guadalquivir. The Carthaginian explorer Hanno makes it to the Gulf of Guinea, and returns home with stories of burning mountains and women covered in fur.

Herodotus reports that the Phoenicians have rounded Africa, with, as footnote, 'something I cannot believe, but perhaps another may'.

In the year 711 after Christ, General Tariq ibn Ziyad crosses to Europe at the head of seven thousand Berber soldiers, to conquer the land of the Visigoths. The current drags at his ships. Rough swells, waves roll solidly, barely fluid, beneath the fleet of *feluccas*; row after row are smashed upon the arid coastline. He lands at the beaches by Gibraltar, the rock that will bear his name: *Jabal Tariq*.

The wind beats at your ears and silences your thoughts. You want to hide from it, from the chill Levanter blowing through the funnel of the Strait.

Navigational instruments improve, and in the Middle Ages there appear portolan charts, showing every shallow and every headland around the Mediterranean; the Strait of Gibraltar, however, is still shunned like the plague. Captains' charts and nautical almanacs may be reliable, but current, wind, and sudden mist are not.

After the Moors are driven out of Europe, British and Dutch merchants begin appearing in the Strait from the sixteenth century — flapping above the harbourfronts of the Mediterranean one sees not only the Venetian lion, the Genoan cross, and the Ottoman crescent, but also the Union Jack and the tricolour of the Republic.

The inland sea becomes a European sea. Shipyards everywhere; countless vessels raise anchor, triumph, are sunk or destroyed by storms. Just as one cannot apprehend all those beautiful horses devoured by the ogre of war, neither can one fathom the ships that go down, the shattered galleys, caravels, galleons, and windjammers — the seabed waits for them patiently.

With the help of the Dutch, the British conquer the

Rock of Gibraltar in 1704 and never relinquish it again. Napoleon, Mussolini, and Generalissimo Franco stare at it till their eyes water; stoically, the British hunker down further into their rock.

After the Second World War — twenty-seven submarines alone are sent to the bottom of the Strait — the merchant ships return. Cruise ships follow. A tinkling glass of gin and tonic in hand — 'Easy on the T, please ...' — the passengers roll through the Pillars of Hercules and then on past the ruins of Carthage, Troy, and Knossos.

Gibraltar is unsuited for mass tourism, although the Rock itself is an attraction and the conditions at Tarifa a drawcard for windsurfers. In spring and autumn, the Strait is a corridor for migratory birds — tourists from around the world stand oohing and ahing from behind their binoculars and tele-lenses.

On the far side, along the African coast, migrants from Morocco and sub-Saharan Africa await their chance to cross. Europe lies in plain sight: on a clear day, white buildings stand out against the rocky coast. So close, just one little leap ...

They come in clapped-out fishing boats and even in truck tyre inner tubes; since the turn of the century, a few thousand of them have drowned in the Strait. In Ksar es-Seghir, a fisherman looks out over the high waves and sighs: 'Around here, you're more likely to find a corpse in your net than a fish.'

On the far shore, in the cemetery of Santo Cristo de las Ánimas in Tarifa, a corner behind white pickets has been reserved for the nameless dead who wash ashore. Tufts of hardy grass bend beneath the wind. A column of vultures and storks rides the thermal, round and round, in endless orbit. Far below, the flash of a ship — the ferry from Tangier to Algeciras.

1

The girls on the top deck brush the hair from their faces. The hazy blue mountain ranges, rising on both sides of the Strait. The places you will never go, the life there. Ilham's eyes wander over the mountains of the Rif, the country they are leaving behind. Why did they stay so long in Rabat? They had the car — they could have gone south, to the desert, but instead they spent the whole time hanging around the city. The terrace at Café Maure; the view of the Bou Regreg estuary and the Atlantic Ocean behind. The boys. The contraband at the boats.

It feels like a loss, that they didn't go to the desert, like a missed opportunity. They could have asked Saleh to go along; women in Morocco rarely travel alone. The looks, the comments — if it remains at that.

They've been on the road for six weeks now, two weeks longer than planned. There had been problems. Situations. Those are behind them now; most of them have been solved.

Saleh comes towards them, holding onto the benches to keep from being knocked over by the pounding of the ship and the hard wind.

The other passengers are downstairs in the salons. Men are sleeping with their legs up on the worn benches; children are fussing, watched over by the women, their fatigue bottomless. The vague smell of piss everywhere.

The freedom on the top deck is better, in the lee of the pilothouse as much as possible.

'*Hola, chicas*,' Saleh says.

'Have you taken a look at him?' Ilham asks.

He nods. 'No worries.'

She is on unfamiliar ground; she has to trust him. His almond eyes, the domineering curl of his lips; you want to believe him.

Fahd shows up too. He stumbles towards them across the deck, in his wake a boy they've never seen before. Fahd slides up beside Saleh, and the new boy sits down beside Thouraya. A long, nasty face, yellow teeth his lips can't quite cover. He produces a hipflask, pours whiskey into the opening of a cola can.

'Who are you?' Ilham asks. She leans over. The wind

tugs at the words in her mouth.

'Mo,' Saleh says. 'He's a gas.'

'Can't he talk for himself?' She sees Mo's Adam's apple bob up and down as he drinks.

The cola can goes round; the girls pass.

'He's riding with me,' Fahd says.

'Oh really?' Ilham says.

'Cheaper than going alone.'

Fahd can't get his cigarette lit, not in the hollow of his hand, not in the shelter of his coat either.

Ilham turns her head and looks at the crests, the sandy-coloured Spanish land beyond. Her mood has swung. Something has been disturbed. The order of things. They started off the day with the three of them, Thouraya, Saleh, and her, united in a conspiracy to get Murat to the far side. First they picked him up in Témara, in Tangier harbour number five; Fahd showed up — he was going to take the spare tyre back to Holland. Murat had nestled down into the deep hollow made for it, where he would spend the crossing, in the dark, covered with baggage. And now, suddenly, there are six of them. That's not good. She was born on the fifth of January. There are five people in her family. The star on the Moroccan flag has five points. Five is better than six. The Israeli flag has six points, and her father hates the Jews.

They light cigarettes from the one Fahd finally got lit. Thouraya snaps her fingers.

'Woof,' Fahd says, and hands her a cigarette. Ilham asks him for one too.

She sucks smoke into her lungs. She thinks about cancer. Her uncle died of cancer. From the steel mills, her father says, but as a matter of fact there isn't a single photo in which he's not smoking a cigarette.

It's her uncle's fault that she was born in Holland. In 1975, her father arrived in France from Targuist — that was all fairly easy back then; his brother convinced him to travel on to Holland. They worked in shifts at the Hoogoven mills, and shared a room in Beverwijk. They married and were laid off during the steel crisis in the early eighties. Life beat them down. Her uncle rose to his feet again, her father remained lying; he was the weaker of the two. But her uncle is dead and her father is still alive.

Sometimes she thinks about life as a *française*. What it would have been like. A big country, more air. The way she's sitting on deck now, the sky high and spacious above her.

She hears her friend say: 'Hey, give me a little room, would you?'

Mo grins and puts his arm around Thouraya. A mouth made for saying dirty little things.

'You they'd like to marry,' Thouraya had said to her sometime in the last weeks. 'With me they only want to do dirty shit.'

Ilham had looked at her when she said it. Thouraya probably meant well, she figured, and she said: 'They'd marry a dog, if it had a Dutch passport.'

Thouraya pushes the boy's arm away. 'Buzz off, man!'

Ilham looks at Saleh. No counting on him. She slides up a few feet, Thouraya slides along with her.

The boys laugh about it. That's the way it works, Ilham thinks, their earnest little game; they can't not do it. Their desire, their eagerness — it has to be on display all the time, it determines their position in the group. They want it, the girls do, they just don't know it yet. They have to be told that they want it.

When he slides up to her again, Thouraya stands up resolutely and says to Ilham: '*Yallah.*'

The other boys talk her into sitting back down; he'll cool it now, really.

A bit of ash blows into Ilham's eye. She dabs at it with the tip of her sleeve.

Saleh is sitting sideways on the bench, looking back at the land they're leaving. She knows he has plans to go back, to set up something there — a boy like him probably has more of a chance in Morocco. The words 'detention centre' and 'repeat offender' wouldn't be hanging in orbit around his life there. Going back — that had been their parents' dream. Everything they did and did not do was a part of going back on that day. That day that never came.

Saleh fishes a joint from the seam of his Gucci cap. The smoke stays inside him for a long time, finally leaving his nostrils in thin, blue streams.

He has said that there's nothing for them to worry about. They don't check passenger cars. They could never do them all. Vans, campers, okay, but not passenger cars.

He has done this before, he says. He'll check on him during the crossing. Bring him a bottle of water, that kind of thing.

The first time she met him was at a wedding party in Rijswijk. She started hearing things right away. Seven months for putting a retarded girl to work for him; he would wait for her at the gate to the shelter and bring her back in plenty of time. It took a long time for them to find out about it.

It could be true, or not, but for a rumour there were an awful lot of details. You couldn't forget about it, but you could look past it; it always remained somewhere at the edge of your vision.

In Rabat, not long after they got there, he had taken her and Thouraya under his wing. He knew his way around. The Andalusian gardens in the Casbah, the cafe perched high on the city wall above the estuary, and the old pirates' nest of Salé, further along, across the river. He kept the boys at bay. At bakers' stands in the Casbah they had seen hornets teeming over the sugar-coated croissants; that's how it was with the boys, too.

The ones from Holland were the only ones Saleh let through. Daoud from Venlo, Brahim who drove a BMW. Even though they were in their parents' homeland and staying with relatives, even though they identified with the people there, they were not Moroccans. That is what they had in common. That they were seen as tourists. That they paid tourist prices. They were the children of two kingdoms, they carried the green passport of the *Royaume du Maroc* and the red-lead one of the Kingdom of the Netherlands, but in both countries they were, above all, foreigners.

The discussions in the playground back then, or in the auditorium — how she had demanded her rightful place. Ilham Assouline, as Dutch as they came. How she had fired personal particulars at them: I, Ilham Assouline, born in the Red Cross Hospital in Beverwijk, a student at Kennemer College high school, who swims in the same dull sea you do in the summer. So if that hasn't made me Dutch already, when will it?

She had been angry and expectant; antagonism only egged her on.

Then two planes drilled their way into the heart of the Western world.

She watched as the little opportunity, the crack that had posed a possibility, sealed over; people looked away and kept their distance, as though her body had, from one day to the next, become a hostile object. The discussions ground to a halt, the bellicose language of the daily news trickled into everyday life. Either you are with us, said the most powerful man in the world, or you are with the terrorists. The plans, his words — they broke her world, the whole world, in two, into *we over here* and *them over there*. And Ilham became *them*. And her body became *over there*. She felt how the enmity nestled in her organs, how she became infected by the fear and the aversion of others. That is how she became what others thought they were seeing, a double transformation.

Ilham Assouline had become a bad name.

2

Algeciras. The ship nears the harbour, tucked back into the bay. Container wharves, freighters. The vast Spanish land behind. Cranes poke into the electric-blue sky. From the trip over, Ilham remembers the nerve-wracking swarm in the passenger terminal, the chaos there; the gates of Africa.

A voice over their heads says it is time to return to their cars.

They trundle down the metal stairs. The ship's engines resonate in the bannisters, the walls, the floors. The car deck is low and dark; many of the sodium lamps are broken. Everyone clambers around the cars, parked with only inches between. They stand on bumpers and trailer hitches, and keep their balance with a hand on the low ceiling. Shouting, always shouting. Engines are started. Ilham chokes, the exhaust fumes bite at her airways, she has a hyperactive gag reflex. She follows Saleh and Thouraya between the cars; the other two have vanished.

Behind the windshields, the motionless fisheyes of men at the wheel, alone with their desires. She thinks about the emaciated stray dogs on the patch of lawn in Rabat, the one on top of the other, his hips trembling back and forth. Thouraya saw it too and laughed. Ilham remembers the desperation in the dog's eyes: something overpowering had taken possession of him, he suffered. The bitch yelped and turned her head to snap at him, but he was beyond her reach.

Everything multiplies exponentially beneath the burning sun. Flies, dogs, people, bacteria in the meat hanging outside in the alleyways. The stomach linings of cows hanging in bluish strips, the flayed carcasses of rams, testicles still attached. One day she had vomited briefly and violently next to a pile of rotting garbage, beside a gate in the *casbah*; more often she was made only a little nauseous by all the manifestations of poverty she saw. The rotting, the cripples, their wounds, the filth. It was everywhere — it was the natural state of everything.

Sometimes they retreated into the McDonald's, into the coolness there. The world as they knew it, the free Wi-Fi. It was there, one day, that they had run into Saleh; Ilham had recognised him. Amazement and joy at a familiar face so far from home. It was the first time Thouraya had met him; she laid her slender, limp hand in his for a moment. 'What's that you're eating?' she had asked.

Saleh had his mouth full, and pointed to the picture of the McArabia above the counter.

She laughed. 'Oh man, a Morocco burger.'

Thouraya was ballsy; there wasn't much she didn't dare to do.

He took them to a beach outside town. There were girls in bikinis there, and boys in shorts scrounging around, gaunt as shadows. Ilham felt sorry for them, for their doggish suffering; along with her pity came contempt.

Thouraya gleamed like a bottle as she came out of the sea. Her head tilted to one side, she wrung the water from her hair. Polished toenails, mother-of-pearl. Fingernails the same. She knew it. The way she crossed the sand towards them, a performance.

'*Tfoo*,' she said, sinking gingerly onto her towel, 'I thought the water would be warmer than that.'

At Club Amnesia, Saleh shook the doorman's hand

and shuffled in, the girls in his wake. They drank pink ladies and mai tais in no particular order. The boys who came here were different from the ones at the beach — they were prosperous and well dressed — but on the dance floor they still pressed their erections up against you, Thouraya said with feigned dismay.

There were moments when you felt like giving yourself away to a stranger, lightly and free of care. Ilham had tried, she really had tried, but her mother's voice — '*Ya msebty!*' — carried across the water. With her father's rage on its heels.

She danced jerkily. She was made up of two bodies. Her collarbones arched elegantly beneath her skin, her shoulders were slender, and she felt that she had pretty wrists and hands, but the body below the waist did not seem to fit well with the rest. Her hips too round, her legs too short, like a figurine of Venus. She distrusted boys who found that attractive. There was something wrong with them. She was, she felt, her upper body. Anyone who lusted after her lower body lusted after someone else; it had nothing to do with her.

'*Hobi*,' Thouraya said a few days later, when she answered the phone. 'So what's the plan?'

Saleh had befriended them eagerly, and they were keen to be chaperoned by him. He was their guide, their interpreter, their fixer. They moved from place to place in their far-too-expensive car, an Audi A4, rented on impulse, just as the whole idea of going to Morocco had been an impulse. Ilham didn't even have a passport. She had taken her sister's; the photo looked passable. She had no money for the trip — Thouraya had loaned her everything. She didn't even have a phone that worked.

They picked up Saleh close to the Tour Hassan, not far from where they were staying at Thouraya's uncle's home. They drove out of town, Thouraya at the wheel. Hedges of red oleander blossomed on the median strip. Moroccan flags flapped above the parade route. The satellite town of Témara, which supplied Rabat with a stream of inexpensive manpower, had more or less fused with the capital now. At Témara's edge, half-hidden among a stand of cork oaks, was a detention centre about which people spoke only in a whisper. Back in the leaden years, opponents of the king had been tortured there. These days, people said, the prisoners were terrorists. Officially, the centre didn't exist at all. And because it didn't exist, there could be no torturing. A scream no one hears has never been uttered.

—

They drove down the boulevard, the ocean glistening on the right. The gondolas of the big Ferris wheel on the beach hung fixed in midair.

They left the main road, Saleh directing from the backseat. They climbed, and came to a plateau. 'So where are we going?' Thouraya asked.

'Turn in here,' Saleh said. The asphalt became a sandy path beneath the trees. They left the sea behind, and the neighbourhood of white-stuccowork bungalows, all new, with bougainvillea blossoming in the yards, glorious orange, white, purple.

Thouraya slalomed around the potholes.

'I'm going to show you two the real Morocco,' Saleh said. 'The way it really is, *wallah*.' He pointed to where they should park, in the shade of the trees. Through a hedge of head-high reeds they saw an improvised settlement.

The car lock beeped. They entered the shantytown; the reed was a twilight zone, the crossing between the world of the owners and that of the disowned.

They passed a firepit where stray cats lay napping dustily in the afterglow. Tyre carcasses and a mattress spring, charred but not consumed; at the edge of the grey ring of ash, bags of garbage were smouldering.

Saleh led the way. The shacks were built of perishable material, wood, plastic sheets — prey to any storm.

Corrugated roofs held in place by car tyres, chunks of cement, broken ceramic tajines, television sets. The houses were huddled together; Ilham peeked inside as they passed. How did these people live? How *could* you live like this, for god's sake?

Here and there, rocks had been used to fashion flowerbeds. Hibiscus and bougainvillea, just like the newly built houses beyond the reeds. Seedlings were sprouting in plastic bottles.

They followed Saleh between the houses, through the maze of alleyways. Thouraya, with her Miu Miu sunglasses and a rose-pink D&G bag over her shoulder, looked like a film star on her way to do charity work.

Where was Saleh taking them? Ilham didn't like surprises. They tended to turn out badly. She drank the last bit of water from her bottle. She couldn't stand the poverty, the heat, and the dust. It exhausted her. There was compassion in her, but beneath the surface also the conviction that poor people had only themselves to blame for living like this. A kind of payback for something. That thought bore her up a little, made it easier to tolerate what she was seeing.

Saleh stepped aside and let Thouraya go first through a low doorway. They entered a room, painted green, with a ceiling as low as the door. Seated on the *sedari* was an old woman with deep-set eyes, surrounded by a swarm of children. The mother animal in the midst of all. Weathered feet stuck out from beneath her skirts; she placed them on the carpet and rose with a sigh. She kissed her visitors' hands and raised them to her furrowed brow. Old tattoos, a pattern of lines and dots. A cascade of greetings in Tamazight. It made them blush; they took her hand and said, '*Shokran, shokran.*' She seemed to be the grandmother of a few of the children, though it was impossible to tell which ones. The children ran in and out. From behind the curtain in the doorway new ones appeared; they stared at the visitors for a while before disappearing again. The old woman left the room; the curtain blew closed behind her.

They sat down on the low sofas. The television was playing loudly.

'Don't be afraid, sweetheart,' Thouraya said to the little girl beside her, who was staring at her wide-eyed. On the television was a bald kung-fu monk with a symmetrical face. 'National Geographic Abu Dhabi', the title in the upper-left-hand corner said. The fighting monk shot like an orange flame across the Manhattan skyline.

Ilham's uneasiness grew. What were they doing here? Who were these people? Saleh's friends? Family? A timid young man entered; he wore a t-shirt that read 'Energie Cottbus'.

'This,' Saleh said, 'is Murat.'

'*As-salamu alaykum*,' the young man said.

'*Alaykumu s-salām*,' Saleh replied. They stood. A hand of skin and flesh, no sinews. He had a handsome face, she thought, with perfect eyebrows. When he smiled, she saw his ruined teeth. The boys exchanged a few words, and Murat disappeared out the door again. Ilham was about to ask Saleh for an explanation when the old woman appeared from behind a curtain and settled back down on the *sedari*.

'Saleh?' Ilham said in a tone that barely masked her irritation. 'Are you going to tell us what we're doing here?'

He lay back on the sofa and began tickling one of the little girls. Be patient, he gestured with his free hand.

The monk made way for *Tom and Jerry*.

Murat came back with a serving tray with glasses, a pot of mint tea, and saucers with dates, pastries, and cactus fruit. He knelt and placed the tray carefully on the table, then poured the tea from a modest height.

'A Moroccan,' Saleh said solemnly, 'will share even the last of his food with you. No matter how poor he is.'

Even he, Ilham thought, didn't consider them Moroccans. 'Murat,' she asked, '*parlez-vous français?*'

He shook his head, a smile of regret playing at his lips. He lowered the teapot carefully and said: '*Pas bien, madame.*'

'*Un peu, peut-être?*'

He nodded. Again, that shy smile.

'*Qu'est-ce que vous faites comme travail?*' The French she remembered from secondary school.

He didn't understand. He looked at Saleh.

'You know, what kind of work does he do,' she said quickly.

Murat listened attentively to the translation. His hand swept back and forth in negation.

'No work here,' Saleh said. 'There's nothing here.'

Ilham nodded and asked no further.

Saleh started tickling the girl again, and said over the sound of her laughter: 'He worked somewhere in France. They busted him.' He spoke to Murat, then said: 'In the Languedoc, he says. As a — what do you call that — *commerçant*?'

'Salesman, or something,' Ilham said.

'He polished crystals for tourists. After a year, they kicked him out.'

The old woman kept nodding the whole time, as though following the conversation closely.

'So how old is he?' Ilham asked. 'He seems so young.'

Nineteen, Saleh figured. He lifted the little girl off his lap and put her on the ground. When she jumped onto him again, the old woman shouted at her to behave.

The pastries were tasteless. Saleh sat up straight and said: 'The Idrissis are very poor. France was their chance. It was really bad luck that he got picked up there.' His gaze moved silently from Ilham to Thouraya. Ilham sensed what was coming. 'They need us,' he said. 'We're here to help each other, right?'

How long has he been working up to this? That was Ilham's only thought.

'It's really easy,' he said. 'We take your car. Murat in the trunk, stuff piled on top of him, and that's it. Lots of Moroccans cross like that. It happens all the time.'

Ilham shifted on the sofa uneasily; everyone in the room was looking at them.

Saleh's voice: 'It's easy, really. I've never been checked, I swear to god.'

'Saleh,' Ilham said quietly, 'you can't do this.'

'In our car?' Thouraya said. 'We can't do that.'

'I've done it so often,' Saleh said.

'What are you, a smuggler or something?'

Ilham shook her head. The old woman got up off the sofa and sank to her knees in front of her. The tattooed crosses, dots, and lines on her face must have been put there an eternity ago; the ink had faded to a pale blue and blurred beneath the skin. The woman seized Ilham's calves and begged.

'We have to help these people,' Ilham heard Saleh

saying. 'Take a look around. We can't just leave them like this, can we?'

The old woman's laments mixed loudly with the soundtrack of *Tom and Jerry*. She took Ilham's hand and rubbed it against her face, her temple. The closeness of that strange, ancient body; Ilham shivered. She realised what she represented to the old woman — a last resort, a way out, a future — and was ashamed. If her own parents hadn't risked the crossing, she might be in the same situation as this woman on her knees, this desperate family that *smelled* of poverty. A bitter feeling of guilt rose up in her — she, the ingrate, who had been given every chance in life, was now denying that to someone else.

Murat spoke. He went on longer than before; this was his plea. His voice was quiet, compelling. The grievous bearing of the martyr.

'He is prepared,' Saleh translated, 'to do anything for the two of you if you take him along. He prays to Allah that you ... that we will take him along. He is grateful for all eternity if you give him that chance. He ...'

The old woman rose to her feet and slapped her skinny ribcage with the flat of her hand. She spat out the words.

'What's she saying?' Thouraya asked.

Saleh waited for a moment, then said: 'She says she

will kill herself if we don't take her son along.'

Ilham groaned quietly. 'Tell them we need to think about it,' she said. 'It's dangerous. We've never done anything like this. We just don't know yet. Right, Thour?'

Her friend blew into her glass and said: 'The car isn't ours, you know? We rented it. If we get caught, they'll take the car. What are we going to do then?'

'We won't get caught,' Saleh said.

Thouraya shook her head. 'Fuck off, Saleh. You go to prison for shit like that. I've heard about it.'

'It's the way everybody does it,' Saleh answered angrily. 'Zero risk.'

Ilham stood up. 'We have to go. Really.'

Saleh communicated their thanks, their best wishes; the formalities back and forth took a long time. Murat followed them outside and watched them go. Ilham looked back. He waved.

3

'He'll never fit, you idiot,' Ilham said. They were driving past the white bungalows, back to the sea.

'If we take out the spare tyre he will,' Saleh said from the back seat.

Thouraya glanced over her shoulder and shook her head. 'You ...' she said, rolling her eyes behind the lenses of her big shades.

His million-dollar smile: Saleh Benkassem, made for the grey economy. After a year at bakery school in Wageningen, he had tried his hand as a strawman in the illegal lottery circuit, and at whatever else crossed his path.

Ilham remembered the rumour about the mentally challenged girl. Now they were the ones who had crossed his path, she realised, and he would use them to his own advantage. She felt powerless. He had wormed his way in between them and the rest of the world, and it seemed as though they couldn't take a step without him. As a woman, you had so few alternatives here; they needed him. Also because they were flat broke. They cadged cigarettes from him and his friends; their drinks were paid for. After closing time at Café Maure, Ilham had let Douad touch her breasts for a moment, off in a corner. One evening, on their way to the amusement park down by the harbour, he had fingered her in the dark, between the fishing boats. His fingers were salty; they chafed at her vagina.

It all started, she thought, with that accident on the way down, at the Afriquia service station just outside Tangier. Thouraya had backed into another car. Fixing the damage had used up almost all the money they had.

When they'd told Saleh about it later, he said: '*Seventeen* thousand dirham? Not even half that … Don't trust these skirts around here, man, really.'

Thouraya's uncle, a carpet dealer with shops in Rabat and Al Hoceima, had slipped them a bit of money now and then during the last few weeks. Not enthusiastically, and far too little to get them back to Holland. He was a dripping faucet that refused to open all the way; they didn't dare to ask for more.

—

At Témara, they parked along the seaside drive. People on the beach below were playing pool on outdoor tables. They found a place beneath a parasol; their chairs wobbled on the bed of sharp gravel. Saleh walked off, holding his phone to his ear. A little further along, boys were jumping into the foaming sea, again and again, tirelessly. Ilham looked at them through her lashes, saw their silhouettes in sharp relief against the glare of the Atlantic.

Thouraya's phone rang. 'No way,' she said. Her mother-of-pearl fingernail ticked at the screen.

Unfamiliar numbers and numbers with a Rotterdam prefix were swiped away. Creditors, the car rental agency. They were already almost two weeks late turning it in. They tried not to think about it. Lots of problems went away by themselves if you ignored them. But an Audi A4 with hastily covered-up damage was not quite that easy.

Saleh slid back under the parasol. 'A new plan,' he said.

'Saleh, please,' Ilham said.

He hushed her. 'They have a proposal for you. Something else. All you have to do is hear them out. You can decide for yourselves. Come on, let's go.'

'Saleh!' Ilham said, but Thouraya was already on her feet.

—

Murat and his mother were sitting beside each other on the sofa; the children had disappeared. A fly was strolling across the pastries.

'She is grateful to you for coming back,' Saleh said.

'Tell her we're happy too, or something,' said Thouraya.

'And that we understand all too well,' said Ilham. 'Life here is … well, horrible. But don't say it like that, okay?'

The woman nodded as Saleh interpreted. She spoke to Saleh, pointing at them as she did. He said: 'She is pleased that the two of you are willing to talk about it, about her son, and she has a proposal to make.'

'Saleh!' Ilham hissed.

He gestured to her to be quiet; the old woman was still talking. Then he said: 'She is willing to pay you for it.'

Ilham shook her head. 'But we already said —'

'Thirty thousand dirham. About three thousand euros.'

Thouraya stared at the Koran, encircled by a garland of plastic flowers, on the low table beside the woman.

'In a few days' time, she can come up with a thousand euros. The rest we can pick up in Holland.'

'It's too risky,' Ilham said. 'Why doesn't anyone mention *that*?'

'Because it's not,' Saleh said. 'Come on, I'll show you.' He got up; the others followed him outside, Ilham bringing up the rear.

'It's not okay,' she said as they walked past the shacks. 'Where are they going to get that money?'

'I guess it's worth it to them,' Thouraya said. 'One hand washes the other, and all that.'

She had already made up her mind, Ilham realised.

'Here,' Saleh said a moment later, bending over the car's boot. 'You take this out …' First he pulled out the floor plate to reveal a deep recess in the body. Then he took out the spare tyre, the jack, the emergency triangle, and the other tools, and said triumphantly: 'Look at all that space.'

Now they all peered into the boot.

Murat climbed in and curled up in the hollow. 'Look, he's doing a test run,' Saleh said, sounding pleased with himself. Murat stuck his head out of the trunk and said something that made his mother laugh.

'What's he saying?' Thouraya asked.

'That it's as comfortable as in his mother's belly,' Saleh replied.

'But he won't be able to stay in there very long,' Ilham said.

'Two hours, max,' Saleh said. 'I'll check on him every once in a while. Don't sweat it.'

Murat really did fit all the way inside it, his knees pulled up and his arms crossed at his chest like a pharaoh. Saleh put the floor plate back in place, hiding him completely from sight.

Ilham felt the pressure growing. Their exasperation. Good fortune was there for the taking — she was the only thing still in the way.

'Let me tell you something,' Saleh said. 'Everybody made the crossing at some point — my parents, yours too — and you've got a good life because of it. But you're not willing to help him. What kind of a person are you? You only think about yourself, really.'

The old woman seized Ilham's upper arms and anointed her head with the gratitude of heaven. Her eyes flashed fire; Ilham sweated from shame. Murat pushed the floor plate away and sat straight up, motionless, in the trunk. Saleh and Thouraya looked interestedly at Ilham and the old woman, as though passing a traffic accident at a snail's pace.

The woman had her fingers intertwined like a serpents' nest, wringing out her old heart in front of her.

And Ilham — Ilham gave in.

4

The ship's deep heartbeat slows. The drivers wait impatiently in semi-darkness. The scraping sound of the bow thrusters, like steel cables being pulled through a pipe. A few rows back from the loading doors, they find the car. Thouraya takes the keys from her purse, the alarm lights blink. Before climbing in, they check on Murat. With a click of the smart key, the lid of the boot pops open.

A fleece blanket, a few cartons of cigarettes, a gym bag, two roll-along suitcases — everything they covered him with at the dump in Tangier, after he disappeared into his hiding place. Between the luggage, a hand is sticking out. A hand with blood on it.

Ilham hisses in shock. The hand is damaged. It looks like the hand of an earthquake victim, sticking out of the rubble. The knuckles are raw, the skin scraped off. The dark-blue gleam of bared flesh.

In a panic, they pull everything off of him. Murat must have tried to fight his way out, like a swimmer struggling to the surface for air. The floor plate has been split in two, with superhuman force, but he wasn't able to push aside the baggage on top of it.

The whites of his eyes are stained with blood; he stares up frozenly, breathlessly, a creature unable to be born. His lips are curled back, his teeth bared in an expression of mute horror.

'Holy fuck,' Saleh whispers.

'He's not *dead*, is he?' Thouraya whispers.

No one touches him. Death's contagion.

Then things happen fast. Saleh pushes Thouraya aside and grabs his gym bag from the trunk. The bag slung over his shoulder, he slaloms through the rows of cars, quick as a cat. Before they have realised what is going on, he has disappeared.

A shock runs through the ship as it touches the quay; car engines start. The noise overwhelms them, as though a race has begun. They slam the trunk and jump into the car. Mouths open, panting in fear. Thouraya's hand shakes as she slips the key into the ignition.

'The bastard,' she says. 'What a bastard.'

Ilham is weeping.

'Stop that,' Thouraya says without looking over. 'If they see you like that ...'

Ilham dries her cheeks, her eyes. Her friend slams the flat of her hand against the wheel.

'What if they find him?' Ilham asks.

'How should I know? Fuck! How am I supposed to know?' A loud click as she locks the doors from the inside.

The ship grazes the quay. They talk agitatedly, but cannot find a way out. 'First we have to get out of here,' Thouraya says. 'I'm going crazy here.'

'We have to tell them we didn't know,' Ilham says. 'That he hid in the car without us knowing about it.'

'No way. I'm not going to prison for that asshole.'

The relief that act would bring, Ilham thinks — '*Señor*, look, a dead boy ...' They wouldn't have to decide about anything anymore; everything would just happen.

Her thoughts fly in all directions. She can't organise them. There is no room for strategy — there is only good luck or bad.

I was right — that is the thought bouncing around in Ilham's mind. I should never have given in.

She can't believe that Saleh really took off. Nobody could be that disloyal. He's gone to his friends, to Fahd, whose Polo is parked halfway back. What is he telling them? What are they saying to him? Congratulating him for having saved his own arse?

'The money ...' she says suddenly.

The money up front. Their travelling money. About a thousand euros in dirhams. Murat had given it to Saleh early that morning, when they picked him up in Témara.

'*Fuck.*' Thouraya rests her forehead on the steering wheel.

Could this really be them, whose lives have turned into a nightmare at the snap of a finger? There is a dead boy in the back of their car, they're going to end up in prison, everything they had in terms of hope, expectations, is ending right here.

The death penalty, Ilham thinks. Do they have the death penalty in Spain?

Saleh had lied to them — he never went to look at the boy. He couldn't have if he'd wanted to; she's suddenly sure that the car deck was locked while the boat was moving.

All they have is a full tank. All the resources they have. How far will that take them?

She flips through the instruction manual for the Audi A4. Distraction. She finds what she was looking for and, with a few pokes and swipes, pins down their position on the navigation screen. 733 kilometres. That's their range with a full tank. From here to Rotterdam, she sees when she punches in the address, is 2460 kilometres.

The drawbridge starts to open, and a strip of light falls onto the deck, like onto the floor of a king's tomb.

Her hands flat against her face, Thouraya is praying. Her lips follow the beaded string of words implanted in her from earliest childhood. Ilham can't remember ever having seen her friend pray before. She herself prays only during Ramadan, on the high holy days. It would be unthinkable for her to refuse.

Thouraya rocks back and forth and murmurs, and then, when she's finished, slides her sunglasses down resolutely onto the bridge of her nose.

The car in front of them begins to move. 'You have to start driving,' Ilham says. She pulls her sunglasses out of her purse, and her eyeliner — she uses the rear-view mirror to tidy herself.

They move with the current. The sound of the wheels on the drawbridge thunders through the car. The swarm is divided over four lanes of asphalt, and crew members gesture wildly and scream as they herd the drivers in the right direction. They move at a snail's pace towards the covered customs shed in the distance.

'We're going to get lucky, baby,' Thouraya mumbles.

Ilham can feel her heart. She never feels it otherwise. It's pounding in her chest and in her ears. Her sister's passport, she realises; they're going to see it! Oh, the stupid, careless way she took off ...

She licks her lips. The metres creeping by. A few vans have been pulled over, an old Toyota Carina. Customs officials are hanging around it, their movements dragging in the heat. *Aduanas*. Power looks at you with cold eyes. Everything shrivels. Your car, your ragged belongings, yourself. Silent and jittery, the children on the Toyota's back seat peer out the windows.

Moroccan families stand beside the vans, worried because authority has turned its gaze on them and not on all those others crawling past them relievedly. Ilham feels ashamed of the family in the Toyota, of their chaotic appearance, of their being so very *African* — they seem so out of place on the continent where they have just set foot.

The customs men don't wave you past, they simply ignore you. Two cars in front of them, a Mercedes is pulled out of the line.

'Okay, baby,' Thouraya says, 'here we go.' She puts on her film-star face, and in a soundless dream they cruise past the customs officials, left and right. Before them, suddenly, there are twice as many lanes of asphalt.

'Was that it?' Ilham hears her own strange, high voice.

Her friend steers concentratedly, her knuckles white

on the wheel. Slowly, they pass docks and warehouses, long lines of trucks with their noses pointed towards Africa. Cars pass them on both sides, Moroccans returning to their countries, cars with French, German, or Dutch plates.

Thouraya says quietly: '*Shokran Allah, shokran Allah, shokran Allah.*'

Where will they be 733 kilometres from now? Ilham does the silent arithmetic. She comes up 1727 short. She looks back. The port has almost disappeared from sight. 'Take it easy now,' she says.

She sees the heartbeat beneath Thouraya's delicate skin, at the side of her neck, like a lizard's pulse. 'We're doing this together,' she says. 'You and me, Thour ...'

Thouraya takes her hand and lays it against her cheek. 'We sure are.'

At a Shell station, the first one they see, they park in the shade of the adjacent restaurant. There is a big Charlie Chaplin on the roof. Inside, a girl places a menu on the Formica tabletop. Thouraya is holding her phone to her ear. 'Fuck him, to hell and back,' she says then, and lays the phone on the table.

'*Huevos,*' Ilham says, keeping her eyes on the menu,

42

'aren't those …' She hesitates, and says: 'Eggs?'

Thouraya tries again. 'He's turned it off, the prick.'

'How much have you got left?' Ilham asks.

They put all their money together. A few banknotes, the coins from the bottom of their purses. The change Thouraya got back in Tangier after they'd filled the tank. All added up, about a hundred euros.

The waitress comes back to their table. They apologise, sweep the money together, and leave the restaurant. In the service station itself they buy two cans of Red Bull. Their thoughts spin like dying flies. They go outside, into the yellow heat. The traffic howls and thunders.

'What,' Ilham says, 'if he's not completely dead?'

'No way. I'm not going to take another look.' Thouraya aims her gaze at the distance, to where the traffic is coming from the harbour. They were there when Saleh and Fahd agreed to meet up, at the first service station outside Algericas. It could still happen. A miracle could still happen; the boys, the money, deliverance. But all they see are truck drivers on slippers and a father with a handful of popsicles. A woman in a headscarf, carrying bottles of water to a car.

They climb in. Thouraya drives to the end of the parking lot, past the trucks and trailers. She stops the car there.

Ilham frowns.

'You wanted to take a look at him, right?' Thouraya says. 'So take a look at him.'

Ilham shakes her head in bafflement and climbs out. Trucks wail as they go by. The soft asphalt beneath her feet, her hand on the lid of the trunk, which Thouraya has popped open from inside the car. Enormous light falls on the parts of his body that had wrestled free. The Energie Cottbus t-shirt has slid up, almost to his dark, nearly black nipples.

'Murat?' she says quietly.

She lifts a suitcase off his legs, frees him from the rest of the baggage. She tosses the broken floor plate into the yellowed grass. His twisted limbs stick out of the oval recess; they look battered, like a violated grave.

'Murat?'

She leans over and holds her hand in front of his mouth. She uses her wrist to feel at his lips, her senses keen. Move, she thinks, breathe. Please.

His eyebrows have been mussed in the scramble. With a fingertip, she smooths the little black hairs. His struggle had been silent, muffled by the floor plate, the luggage, the lid of the boot. Ship's engines drown out his muted signs of life. No one hears his shouts. Each scream cinches his breath in further. He wrestles with the luggage on top of him, pounds at the lid of the trunk; he can't free his legs to kick at it and force the lock. He has only a trunk full of oxygen, and his lungs lock quickly in a vacuum. Every effort brings the end nearer. There is no pain, only fear. Clawing, gasping for air, he sinks to the bottom of the sea. Blessed be the oblivion — a godsend is death.

5

They drive east, sunlight stretched across their upper legs. Estepona, Marbella, the sea is never far. The Cordillera Bética rises up on their left, hazy in the afternoon light. Ilham's winded breathing. 'His mother,' she says. 'Someone has to tell her.'

'Saleh.'

'You think so?'

'No.'

Trucks crawl up the incline.

'He'll go back and cash in on the rest,' Thouraya says, 'and they'll never hear from him again.'

Ilham nods. 'It's the mother's fault too, actually,' she says then. 'She more or less *forced* him into it. Her own son. Can you imagine?'

'She had to do something, right?'

'Yeah, and now he's dead.'

'She knew the risks. So did he.'

A burl in briarwood, tough as iron, Thouraya. The axe hits and sticks. The flash of anger in Ilham. You were just as keen about it, she feels like shouting, but bites her lip. After all, Thouraya would only say, you agreed to it too, didn't you …?

In the end, yes, in the end.

The rusty soil here is pocked with scrub. The road rises and drops. Málaga, 126 kilometres. They follow the coast, no plan in mind. At Málaga they will turn north, that's all they know, following the caravan route of their parents into the killing heat of the Spanish plateau. Like those summers in the past, lolling in the back of the packed van with their brothers and sisters, their clammy legs, the drops of sweat on their noses.

Thouraya's father, her friend had told her as they drifted over endless asphalt on their way down, couldn't read; he had simply followed the cars of friends and family on their route south. That was how they got to Algeciras. Everyone knew the stories about robbers along the way, bandits pretending to be policemen. That was why they travelled in a convoy of a few cars; at the rest areas along the highway they stood close together, like covered wagons in Indian territory.

At the harbour, it was the customs men.

Even as a young girl, Thouraya had looked down on her father. He was, she felt, as tough as he was stupid. She had inherited the former from him. He knew what it was to bear up. He bore up under the scraping of tanker holds in the harbour and a family with six children when he got home, his wife as she pined away. His own father, in turn, had borne up under the years of starvation in the Rif, when the birds fell dead from the sky. She knew the stories about the people who, before they could reach the city, were buried where they fell beside the road. Time had erased the stories' sharp edges — only the solid core remained, a volcanic monolith: the suffering, the hunger, the dying.

When you see her, you can't help but realise that she is proud of being a Berber, hard and rough as the mountains of her forefathers. But she looked down on her father. His endurance was that of a beast that did as it was told, and that bore up until its legs buckled and collapsed.

One day he had fallen forty feet and shattered his hip. 'God was out to kill him, but got the height all wrong,' Thouraya said. Drawn into the gearwheels of the labour-disability machine, he lived on to terrorise his family in their single-storey flat in Delfshaven.

The first time she ran away from home, she was sixteen. She did it two more times before leaving for good. She preferred the shame of the family's lost honour to a forced marriage. While staying at the young women's shelter, she took the opportunity to finish high school; she now worked as a beauty consultant at a salon on Nieuwe Binnenweg in Rotterdam, where she fitted Cape Verdean and Caribbean women with hair extensions and long nails. Someday she was going to start her own hair and nail salon. That was how her future looked: a strictly materialistic vision.

The road's surface shimmers in the afternoon heat. It is thirty-six degrees out. Whenever Thouraya smokes a cigarette she opens the window a crack. Her hair floats up in the rush of hot air.

'So what are we going to do, Thour?'

'You're asking me?'

'I can't ask him.'

Thouraya grimaces. 'How should I know? We have to get rid of him, I guess.'

'How were you going to do that? Just dump him along the road somewhere?'

'Why not?'

She's already thought about all of this. The orange lights in the roof of a tunnel slide by rhythmically.

Two highways run parallel along the Costa del Sol; they've taken the southern one, the one with no toll.

It is, Ilham thinks, disgraceful to feel hungry when you're travelling with a dead person. Still, she feels hungry. They've barely eaten a thing since they left Rabat that morning. She can smell her own breath.

Her friend nods. 'We'll stop somewhere in a bit.'

'He was nice,' Ilham says. 'Even though you couldn't really talk with him. He seemed really nice to me.'

'Don't think about things like that. You'll only make it harder for yourself.'

'I can't turn off my mind, can I?'

No reply.

Ilham asks for a cigarette.

'But you don't smoke during the day,' Thouraya says.

'I do now.'

The cigarettes are packed tightly together; she worms one out of formation. She had smoked on board too, while the boy was suffocating in the hold. Her life had been the same back then, his perhaps already over.

Thouraya hooks up her iPod to the car stereo. '*Aïcha.' Comme si je n'existais pas, elle est passée à côté de moi.* She turns up the volume, and Cheb Khaled's fragile voice fills the car. She sings along loudly, as though trying to drown out her thoughts. *J'irai ou ton soufflé nous mène dans les pays d'ivoire et d'ébène.* Thouraya makes sounds without knowing what she's singing, like a child, and Ilham has tears in her eyes because the nice boy's ears will never hear lovely music like this again. *J'effacerai tes larmes, tes peines …*

The coast is built up: gravel drives, hotels. Golf courses of green silk. Every once in a while, a viaduct spanning a mountainside *wadi*. All those dreary tourist lodgings, one after the other, and everywhere the turquoise sparkle of pools. She longs to float, her ears underwater, her closed eyes turned to the sun, to make the heaviness disappear along with the sounds.

Days long ago — the heat of the sun on her skin, the light's embrace. The mesmerised stare at the nimble glistening of water in the pool. What she liked most was to float on her back and listen to phantom snatches of sound, the shout of children's voices, bodies hitting the water. A huge distance between her and the rest. She heard her own deep breathing. She drifted; she was not afraid.

—

At times, they drive right beside the sea. The car parks are full; the high season is running full throttle. Ilham experiences the exhaustion that overtakes her sometimes when she walks into a round-the-clock service station, the fatigue in everything, transferred to her, too.

She sees bathers, their dark heads far out at sea. How will they ever get rid of him? There are people everywhere. Cranes sling their loads through the air; cars, vans, trucks everywhere; it is as though all those eyes can look right through their car. Hey, did you see that dead guy in the back?

The nerve-wracking milling about of people, descending from the mountains to the coast, which they have colonised, occupied, right down to the last square metre. From outer space this coastal strip can be seen as a long, stretched-out haze of stars, jammed between the blackness of the sea and the mountains; in the mountainous interior there glistens only here and there a single, feeble star, surrounded by deep darkness.

Their future consists of a couple of hundred kilometres and scarcely a hundred euros. Never have her chances been so slim. On the far side of those kilometres and euros, a wall looms.

'We could sell the cigarettes,' she says suddenly.

'What?' Thouraya turns down the music.

'We could sell the cartons of cigarettes.'

Thouraya turns the music back up again. She's alone with herself.

Why doesn't she drive a little slower? If they get pulled over, they're done for. Again, Ilham wonders: do they have the death penalty in Spain? Is being an accessory to the boy's death enough to get you the death sentence? How would they carry out that sentence here? She remembers a *sura* about retribution: a soul for a soul, an eye for an eye, a nose for a nose, an ear for an ear, a tooth for a tooth … On Al Jazeera she'd heard that punishments like that were still imposed sometimes: the surgical removal of both eyes for someone who had attacked a woman with acid. She has taken Murat Idrissi's life. She took it by giving in. Her 'yes' was his death sentence. A soul for a soul: symmetrical retribution. He descends from heaven to fetch her. Together they rise up. His teeth are straight and clean.

At Fuengirola they exit to a McDonald's. At the top of the incline, cars tear by on the A-7. The car park is lined with palms and rubber plants. They manoeuvre up to the McDrive.

'Chicken nuggets,' Thouraya says into the intercom. 'And a milkshake. Strawberry.'

A question is asked.

'*Six* nuggets,' Thouraya says, as though arguing with the two-way speaker. She listens intently to the voice coming back, then turns to Ilham. 'They don't have milkshakes — I think that's what she's saying. Ridiculous.'

Then Ilham shouts her order from the passenger seat.

As they wait at the pick-up window, Thouraya says: 'A McDonald's without milkshakes … come on.' And, after she's been handed the paper bag with food and beverages: 'Without milkshakes, they shouldn't even be allowed to call it a McDonald's.'

They find a spot to park the car and unpack their meal. Ilham puts the paper cup of cola down at her feet and unwraps her hamburger. Thouraya stares for a while at the box of chicken nuggets on her lap, then says: 'Hey, I'm not going to sit in here and eat with that in the back.'

She climbs out; the car door slams.

'I'm not scared of you, man,' Ilham says over her shoulder. She eats her hamburger calmly. In the shade, beneath a stretch of canvas that spans the terrace, Thouraya is sitting with the untouched cardboard box on the table in front of her.

We would have been better off buying petrol with this money, Ilham thinks.

She gets out and crosses the road. The heat bites;

she slips under the shade of the canvas. She shakes the ice in her cup, the cola draws a cold trail through her innards. Then she sees it: a light-blue Polo — the boy in the backseat: Mo, with his camel face, looks out the back window at her just as she looks at him, in a moment of extreme sharpness and clarity, then it is over.

'Thour!' she stammers. 'That was them, there! There they are, *there* …' She points; they catch a glimpse of the back of the Polo as it disappears up the ramp towards the highway.

They run to the car. The energising desperation — they have to catch up with them; it's their only chance.

The rotunda, the turn-off, and they shoot back onto the highway. A tourist bus blows clouds of diesel fumes; they can't get past it. Then, with a hard twist of the wheel, Thouraya dives into the tight space between two cars in the left lane. The Audi has the most powerful engine — it can do 280 — but the traffic is skittish. The coast road has one exit after another; it's stop and go. The boys, if that's who it was, might take any exit and lose them for good.

Ten kilometres, twenty kilometres. Fuengirola is far behind them now, and the two highways merge into one. They realise that it's hopeless: they'll never find the boys again. The country is huge and endless, and the roads fan out in all directions.

'I'm positive that I saw him,' Ilham says sheepishly.

They have enough petrol for 450 kilometres. They have almost 2200 to go.

6

The A-7 turns north, and they leave the sea behind. The road lies in the shadow of a leaden mountain range that rises steeply on their left. There is a brief moment of eclipse as they disappear into the mouth of a tunnel, the black second in the transition from light to darkness. Ilham's shudder at the entrance to the underworld. She is alert, her senses heightened.

Thouraya looks at her phone while she's driving; she steers with her knees.

'You're allowed to go a hundred here,' Ilham says.

Thouraya looks up. 'I'll do the driving, okay? I go nuts when you try to tell me how to do it.'

'Well, then, keep at least one hand on the wheel.'

The whites of her eyes. 'What's with you?' She holds the phone to her ear.

'Fuck, Saleh,' she says after a few seconds, looking at the blank screen. 'Fuck …'

They glide over smooth asphalt, black as freshly laid. Vistas once in a while, the revelation of chalk-white settlements in the valleys. Utility towers follow the ridges. The slopes are covered in thousands upon thousands of olive trees, in neat formation, one hill after the next; Ilham never knew there could be so many olive trees.

It's almost five o'clock. The temperature, now that a mountain range separates them from the sea, has risen to thirty-nine degrees.

The illusionless hour, its cheerless light, like a nightclub at closing time.

Thouraya opens the window. She shoves her nose into the current of air. Then she shakes her head and says: 'It's not coming from outside.'

Ilham says nothing. She has smelled it too. His odour drifts through the car like a *djinn*.

'Light a cigarette for me, please,' Thouraya says.

Ilham lights two at once. She inhales deeply. The loud whoosh of the cracked window hurts her ears.

Only for a moment does the smoke drive away the smell. They know it isn't really gone, only waiting to reappear once the cigarette smoke has dispersed.

With each breath they smell his rotting body. Now

that his immune system has shut down, bacteria in his intestines have turned against their host; his dead cells serve as the bacteria's food. The greasy stench seems to stick to everything — it is a *physical* presence. The heat speeds up the decay. The boy has left his body and communicates with them through a ghastly stench. Don't forget me, his smell says.

How Ilham longs for the innocence of the early morning, when they drove out of Rabat. The cool morning, almost motionless, the smells and sounds of the city not yet in motion. They come past the Oudayas Casbah; men pushing rattling handcarts disappear through a huge gate in the medina.

As they drive out of town, Ilham sees a little mosque; masons are busy replastering its ancient walls.

In Témara, the ocean looms like a darkness. Murat is waiting under the trees. He is alone. A minimum of baggage — nothing but a plastic bag, really. He fishes a little bundle of banknotes from his trouser pocket. Saleh counts it, adroit as a moneychanger.

Ilham hears roosters far away and close by; above the hovels hangs a thin mist of woodfires. The smell of smoke gives her a sense of security. At the edge of her conscious mind, memories rise up, mornings like this one — the coolness, the crowing of cocks, the smoke, but they remain with neither time nor place.

The mood in the car is elated. Cigarettes are passed around. Murat is cheerful and talkative. She hasn't seen him like this before. He's beaming; this is his day. Saleh translates only a portion of the conversation they carry on in the backseat.

They take the new toll road to Tangier; there's almost no traffic. The sun comes up in a wash of peach-coloured light. They pass greenhouses and plantations, the fields full of sweet, round watermelons, ready for the harvest. The melons rest nakedly beside their furrows, like eggs the earth has pressed out.

'What is he planning to do in Holland?' Ilham asks. 'Does he know people there or something?'

'He knows how to repair shoes,' Saleh interprets, 'and he can carry loads. Those are always in demand. People who can carry loads.' He nods. 'And he knows us — that's what he says.'

Thouraya sniffs loudly. 'As long as he doesn't come knocking on my door.'

Eucalyptus trees rise up on both sides of the road, bark hanging in melancholy strips from their trunks.

He has long lashes for a boy, Ilham thinks. Maybe someday he'll earn enough to pay for a dentist. Maybe he'll even find a wife — if he sends home for a cousin, for example. She imagines a tightly circumscribed life, rather like that of her own parents. A life constantly on the edge of want, and the eternal complaint that *everything is so expensive in this country* — that even though you may earn more than you would in Morocco, you spend it all right away on a contribution for this or coverage for the other.

At a tollbooth, they wait in line behind a truck loaded with watermelons. Atop the pile of fruit is a boy. He laughs and waves to the vehicles that follow. The truck takes off, rattling loudly in a black cloud of exhaust. Thouraya takes the ticket from the machine, the barrier gate opens, she honks farewell to the boy on the melon truck.

It's tempting to mimic Saleh and Murat's lightheartedness. As though all they're doing is getting up to a bit of mischief, and later, when it's over, they'll all call it *a good gag*. But if you listen carefully you hear traces of their anxiety; it's in the higher tones of their laughter, the quickness of their conversation.

Ilham wishes she were alone with Thouraya, so they could talk about whether they were doing the right thing, whether they weren't doing something incredibly stupid. But for as long as they have been friends, Thouraya has always drawn her into things she would never dare to do herself. 'Don't be such a old biddy' is about the worst thing she can say to you. When Ilham had gone to school to study financial administration — against her parents' will; they figured it was time for her to marry — she had called Thouraya every day. Thouraya was a fantastic scold. The hearty disgust with which she talked about 'those farmers'. 'They just want to keep you as dumb as they are. Well, forget it. It's your life.'

In the fields, the farmers are working the ground with hoes. Most transport here goes by horse and wagon. The occasional donkey. Long-armed spray installations do the watering.

Ilham looks over her shoulder. 'Would you ask him if he's scared?'

'Scared of what?' Saleh asks.

'About later on. The boat. If he gets caught …'

'Il, come on, knock it off.' That's Thouraya.

'I'm just asking.'

'Why should he be scared?' Saleh says. 'He's happy, right? Believe me.'

'He's not afraid of getting caught?'

Thouraya shakes her head.

'So just ask him,' Ilham says to Saleh.

'Ask him what?'

'Whether he's scared.'

'I'm not your slave or something.'

'Okay, just do it,' Thouraya says wearily.

Murat nods once he's understood the question, and speaks directly to her. He talks for a while, and Ilham lets herself be carried along absentmindedly by his flow of words. When he is finished, Saleh says: 'He's not scared. He trusts in Allah.'

'Was that all?' Ilham says. 'Come on, he said a lot more than that!'

Saleh shrugs.

'Saleh, really!'

'Okay, relax … He has some kind of pouch with him. With herbs and stuff. How should I know? His mother got it from the marabou. For good luck — you know what I mean.'

Ilham looks back and forth from one boy to the other, then nods, a sadness tugging at the corners of her mouth. '*Shokran*, Murat. *Shokran*.'

He smiles, showing his grey teeth.

They drive past forests of cork oak. A pouch with herbs and stuff, the life breathed into it by magic … She stares out of the window. The trees flash by. It's the world of her mother, a world she can't accept. It depresses her, the quick prayers whenever death is mentioned, when there are portents. All those dos and don'ts. The countless fears her mother covers up with invocations. The things you're not allowed to say, not allowed to think, not allowed to do. Her mother is a farmwoman — she went to the airport on the back of a donkey, as Thouraya puts it; she has a certain control over the new language. She is fairly independent, but there is no use trying to combat her primitive ideas — her reply is always that her daughter is rude, and that rude girls end up badly.

In her mind, Ilham sees Murat in a room somewhere in Holland, perhaps a room he shares with other men like him. He takes good care of the pouch with herbs and stuff. He may caress it; it will gradually become a substitute for home.

'What was that?' she hears Thouraya say.

'A dead goat or something,' Saleh says.

Ninety more kilometres to Tangier. The sun climbs quickly into the sky. A few times another vehicle passes them, and a wave of pressure pushes their car to one side. A black Mercedes disappears into the distance. He must be doing at least 200 kilometres an hour. A member of the royal family, Saleh says. He makes a clicking noise with his tongue, a sound somewhere between awe and disapproval.

At the side of the road they see the occasional water-melon, rolled off a truck and broken; they make Ilham think of bleeding heads.

The bouncing pickups, loaded with ears of corn, melons and onions, the people in the fields, their deeply chapped hands that will never be clean again, the sun that makes their skin rough and leathery — Ilham realises what kind of life her parents saved her from. She may not be a fully-fledged Dutchwoman, but she is at least certainly a Moroccan 2.0, a coveted object for matrimony.

All her parents ask for in return is obedience. Only that. And she, the ungrateful daughter, denies them that to which they have a right.

7

The truck drivers looked up when they walked into the roadside restaurant. Their gazes swung from Thouraya to Ilham and back again. The bar was covered in saucers, each one waiting with a teaspoon at its edge. The television was showing the football scores. A young woman with an angular face was polishing the crockery, then wrapping the knives and forks in paper napkins. There was a tinkling sound every time she dipped into the cutlery tray. Every once in a while, she paused to take a drag on her cigarette. Smoke coiled up from the ashtray.

They took a table somewhere halfway to the back of the restaurant, beside a window from which they could see a sun-bleached plastic playhouse in a little playground. The swings were swaying gently. Thouraya laid her phone beside her knife and fork, then made a face and snatched it back off the sticky tabletop. She shifted uneasily in her chair. 'Hey. Listen. Smell me, would you?'

Ilham leaned across the table.

'Can you smell it?'

'No,' Ilham said. She shook her head and sank back in her chair. 'Maybe a little,' she said then.

Thouraya blinked her eyes, aghast. 'Pffff … You're kidding, right?'

Ilham could smell it on herself too. It was in her hair, her clothes.

One of the men got up and went out of the door. Light, sharp as a scalpel, entered the room.

The skinny young woman came over to them. She wore white stockings with frills and black patent-leather shoes, like she was taking her first communion.

'I never drink coffee,' Thouraya said. 'But now I'm going to.'

'*Café*,' Ilham said, holding up two fingers.

She had no idea why she'd ordered the same. Maybe to keep the moment of contact as short as possible. Before the waitress smelled it too. Before she smelled it and told the men at the bar that those two over there smelled like a *corpse*, and the men wouldn't be able to keep their eyes off them.

They fell silent. Ilham jumped every time the purple insect lamp crackled, each time another fly was electrocuted.

'We have to get rid of him,' Thouraya said quietly. 'Really.' And a little later: 'What I actually feel like is leaving the whole fucking car right here.'

A grisly undertaking, somewhere over the horizon. Ilham stared at the dust-coloured hills, the wrinkles in the rock, which from this distance looked soft and pliable. Who he was — a son, a brother, a boy with long lashes and slender fingers — didn't matter anymore. He was nothing but a body they had to get rid of. A dead body that dragged them with its stench halfway into the underworld themselves. It had to happen: they had to be rid of him because he already belonged *there* and they still belonged *here*.

It had been the stench, Ilham realised, that finally alienated her from him.

Thouraya lifted the saucer, keeping the cup balanced with her other hand. 'I'm going outside. Oh man, this is so hard for me to take. Really, so hard ...' She was on the verge of tears. She was always so careful to keep herself clean. All right, she didn't pray anymore — you had to be clean for that — but she showered two or three times a day if she had the chance. She washed her hands more often than anyone else Ilham knew. A neurosis inherited from her mother, who turned up her nose at the homeless people in Rotterdam, whose life on the street started with dirty fingernails and ended as human garbage. The homeless were the focal point of her mother's fear of contamination.

The patio was deserted. They sat in the wind that tumbled from the slopes. Ilham was startled by her desperation. 'We'll find someplace,' she said. 'Somewhere away from the road. We'll do it there, okay?'

Thouraya nodded, her eyes on the ground.

Ilham went inside to pay. The drivers glanced up from the television; the waitress had disappeared. Ilham stood at the bar and waited. It took an awfully long time.

'Maria!' one of the men shouted, his eyes still fixed on the screen.

Ilham looked outside; she heard voices and laughter on the patio. Boys — they were talking to Thouraya across the tables. Moroccans, she figured; she heard Dutch.

The waitress appeared from behind the swinging doors, her hands fastening her apron strings behind her back. Ilham slid a ten-euro note across the bar. They were more or less the same age. They looked at each other briefly as she received the change, their eyes searching around in the other.

'*Gracias*,' Ilham said.

'*De nada*.'

At the door, she looked back. The waitress was setting cups on the rows of saucers. '*Hasta luego*,' she said to Ilham, as though passing along a secret message, an SOS for rescue.

Wolves, Ilham thought. There were three of them. One was sitting across from Thouraya, his legs straddling the back of the chair like a cowboy.

'Jesus, Il, take that look off your face.' The transformation was complete. She had pepped herself up to her old, radiant self, ready for action.

'*As-salamu alaykum*, princess,' said the boy on the chair.

'And who might these be?' Ilham asked.

'The Rotter-Damned Posse,' the boy said.

'Maassluis,' Thouraya said. 'Don't let them kid you.'

Ilham could tell by the way she raised her eyes, the little twist at the corners of her mouth.

The boy laughed and ruffled his hair with one hand. '0–10's the code, baby.' He held his head tilted to one side, a frisky dog. Then he introduced Ilham to his friends — 'Driss, Jalal' — and, finally, to himself. 'Noureddine. Noor for you. It looks like we're heading in the same direction.'

'Oh,' Ilham said, 'is that what she's been telling you?'

'We figured,' said the boy whose name was Driss, 'that we could go to some motel later and chill. Spliff, little vodka maybe. That you two could go along. Fun, right?'

'Ugh,' Ilham said, 'you guys are too slick for your own good.'

They had been to the coast; they'd spent almost the whole month of August on the beach and cruising the streets of Nador. They had been on the same boat as the girls. They were taking it easy. 'Tomorrow is another day,' said Noureddine. He laced his fingers together at the back of his head. 'Lectures won't be starting for another week.'

'Well, well, Mr Higher Education,' Thouraya said.

'Is that what they call them these days, lectures, at vocational school?' Ilham asked.

His friends laughed. Noureddine leaned his elbows on his knees and looked at her. There was something like amusement in his eyes, something vaguely superior that she hadn't seen before in boys like him. It made her waver. Her natural defences faltered.

Jalal went in and got drinks, Driss looked at his phone; the sun glistened on the pavement.

'*Hamdullah!*' Driss said suddenly. 'An Etap. Eighty kilometres from here.'

Noureddine sighed contentedly. 'Yeah, man, kickin' back.'

'It's hotter than a witch's tit, *wallah*,' said Driss.

'You wish,' Ilham said.

Thouraya got up. 'Come on, Il.'

'Where are we off to now, ladies?' Noureddine asked.

'Girl stuff,' Thouraya said.

She walked into the cafe, Ilham on her heels.

Thouraya pulled the door of the ladies' room closed behind them and lit into her right away. 'Why are you acting so bitchy? I'm trying to fix this up. I smell like a goddamn' — here she lowered her voice — '*corpse*, I feel filthy, I want to get out of this shit country. They're from Holland, Il, these guys are our ticket — don't you get it?'

'He's a snake, just like Saleh,' Ilham said, intimidated.

'So what? We need these guys. Have you got a better idea? We've got nothing, Il. Zero, *nada*.' She was quiet for a moment. 'Let me fix this. You stay out of it.'

Ilham disappeared into one of the cubicles and shut the door behind her.

'Okay?' Thouraya said.

Ilham could see Thouraya's mother-of-pearl toenails in her gladiator sandals. 'Okay?' she heard her ask again.

'Suit yourself,' Ilham said. She heard the sound of an atomiser. The floral scent of Anaïs Anaïs wafted under the door. 'I'll leave it here for you,' Thouraya said, and went out.

They kept the windows open. The stench was unbearable, but after a few kilometres the dry retching had stopped. In late, gritty light they drove the empty highway, the boys out in front. Driss was driving — it was his car. Sometimes the boys dropped back beside them, showing off, laughing. Noureddine was lying in the back seat, his tanned feet sticking out the window. Thouraya waved.

A hedge of sunflowers ran on for kilometres, their leaves withered and limp, the big flower heads languishing on tall, thin stalks. Then, once again, tunnels and viaducts across deep ravines; for a while, the road followed a dry riverbed in the depths. At the end of the pass a high plateau opened before them, the catchment area of the Guadalquivir.

They turned off at an *area de servicios*. The city

coming up, Ilham saw, was Jaén.

Thouraya parked the car far away from the boys. She spritzed a bit of perfume on herself and handed the bottle to Ilham. Behold the female of the species, approaching the pack across the hot asphalt. It was second nature to Thouraya; somewhere in early puberty she had realised that the erotic economy was a promissory one. Keeping a little fire going, sometimes a few little fires at once. Stirring it up a bit, blowing softly across the coals now and then. Sometimes you didn't have to do anything at all.

A chain restaurant. A little further on, at the end of the parking lot, the Etap hotel, rectangular as a domino.

Ilham was reconciled to her role as the beauty's friend. She didn't want anything from them. On the patio behind the restaurant she drank cola through a straw and stayed out of everything — the conversation, the hormonal stuff. Only when Noureddine spoke did she assay him quickly, as though listening to him. He had the grin of a Bedouin on horseback. His hair was not short and trimmed up tight at the sides, like most Moroccan boys had it, but full and gleaming. His existence ran of its own accord. He was desired. By friends, women, by life itself. Ilham knew girls who were like that. A couple of them, not many; graceful, subdued creatures with long fingers. Even their knees

74

were pretty. Boys like that were even rarer. Gijs Loman was the only one she could think of. From the first year of secondary school, they'd had what they called an 'intellectual friendship'. They talked about politics and culture; sex and gossip were inferior. She was the one who watched over the ground rules, and only rarely did anything intrude.

She kept the existence of Gijs Loman a secret from her parents. They would have pulled her out of school right away if they'd known she was seeing a Dutch boy. Her mother reminded her regularly and laboriously of the gap between the Dutch and Moroccans — the idiotic *huma hollandiyen, wa hna mgharba* was etched into her consciousness — it was a chasm that was not to be bridged.

It ended when he was scouted and went to play field hockey for Bloemendaal. He started on an elite sports curriculum, and so she saw him only rarely. All that time she had been in love with him, she realised, and had hidden it away beneath grave conversation.

Darkness crept into the valley. Two women on a bench watched silently over their children in the fenced-in playground. Demonstrative Spanish faces. The playground equipment was built on a substrate of soft, bilious-green astroturf.

Gijs Loman seemed like centuries ago; it was as though the hope and energy of her schooldays had deserted her, and she had been expelled for good from the world she'd once wanted to be a part of so badly. The only Dutch people she saw these days were at the call centre where she worked, in the basement room where she spent her days looking at feet and ankles passing on the pavement outside, while her lips, tickled by the mike's foam cover, paid service to savings plans. Her life was slipping backwards, she felt, while those of her former classmates and college friends kept moving on. Or maybe it wasn't so much that her life was slipping backwards but *under*wards, if you could even say that; she was sinking slowly into the deep, and looking up from below at the rush of human legs. She drifted further and further away from the others, tired and defeated.

At times, she wasn't all that far from giving in — all she had to do was nod and her life would take on its form. Before she knew it, there would be a Moroccan Dutchman at her side, she would have henna tattoos on her hands, and she'd be a watermelon on stilts. Even though her husband had sworn he was as modern as the next man, it wouldn't be long before they'd be having arguments about the wearing of the hijab. And that would be her last argument. After that she would still experience moments of rage and desperation, but generally speaking it was better this way, quieter and better. That's the way it had gone with her mother and with her grandmother, and all those women before them whose bones had long ago been absorbed by the stony soil of the Rif.

8

From the patio, she could see, amid the olive orchards, the orange roofs of the oil presses. The waiters never ventured outside. Ilham touched her tongue furtively to the salt on her wrist. Had they remembered to lock the Audi? Was that the beep of the alarm she heard? The thought would not leave her be; after a few minutes, Thouraya absent-mindedly handed her the key.

Ilham walked through the restaurant and shivered in pleasure at its coolness. There were goosebumps on her skin.

Still a way off from the car, she pushed the lock button and the warning lights flashed. The sun had withdrawn behind the hills, but the asphalt was still giving off its heat. Darkness washed over the mountains they had come across; cars rolled up from the pass and disappeared in the direction of Jaén, the beams of their headlights leading them into twilight. She breathed easier, now that she was alone. She didn't feel like going back to the others already; sweat droplets tickled the back of her neck as she walked towards the hotel, across the big car park from the restaurant. The glass doors slid open for her without a sound. The man at the reception desk took his eyes off the computer screen and nodded. The hotel was plain and utilitarian: there was a dispensing machine with soft drinks and sugar-coated croissants in cellophane, and a coffee machine beside it. A sign told her the rooms were air-conditioned. She longed for a bed. To bury herself in cool, impersonal linens. But first a long shower, and then she would find Thouraya in the room, smoking a cigarette beside a wall ventilator and wrapped in a towel, and then swearing to each other that it was all going to turn out fine. Everything, all of it.

She walked back. The air on the lot was searing, as though she were breathing fire.

Jalal was walking towards her across the asphalt. He was, he told her, going to reserve two rooms, before they got too plastered and had to sleep outside.

'Two?'

'One for us and one for you two, right?'

Ilham shrugged.

He laughed. 'But you never know.'

As she was about to walk on, he grabbed her by the shoulder. 'Come with me — you're not going to let me go alone, are you?'

She twisted away from his grasp. 'You're a grown man.'

He didn't press the point.

On the patio they were eating little, deep-fried fish. 'Try some,' said Noureddine. He stuck a few in his mouth and licked his fingers. Dark, the trees on the surrounding slopes. Fresh drinks were brought from inside. Ice cubes tinkled, condensation trickled down the glass. Ilham took a vodka from the tray and drank it, holding her breath.

'Here, have some of these,' Noureddine said. He squeezed some lemon onto the plate and held it up to her.

She ate. Her hands went from plate to mouth and back. The fish bones crunched between her back teeth.

When he laughed, she was startled. 'Doesn't matter,' he said. 'We'll order another plate.'

She felt ashamed. Why was he being so nice? What did he want? It was all so unclear; she couldn't think straight. That morning she had seen the Atlantic, and then, along the toll road to Tangier, the light between the eucalyptus trees, the start of a majestic sunrise; a country and a lifetime ago.

Thouraya asked what he was studying, and then, when he replied 'political science', whether he wanted to be a politician.

'God, no.' He laughed. 'I don't want to have power, I want to find out how power works. Machiavelli, Tocqueville — that mean anything to you? Doesn't matter.'

Driss grinned. 'Aye, man, Tupac is Machiavelli. Brad Pitt, ask them about Brad Pitt — they've heard of him.'

'Sure,' Thouraya hissed. 'Not like you had any idea.'

'Women, never underestimate them, fuckbucket,' Noureddine said.

Again, that irritation. Why did everything he said sound like he was reading it out loud?

Driss picked up his phone and tapped the recorder, holding it up to his mouth. 'Over and under, es-ti-mate …' he rapped.

Ilham pursed her lips, looking impressed.

'Come on,' Noureddine said. 'Tocqueville, anyone?'

Thouraya's expression was noncommittal. Driss was working on his recording.

Noureddine shook his head. 'What am I going to do with you people?'

He turned his gaze on her. 'Ilham, you know what I'm talking about.'

She shrugged. 'Only from hearsay.'

'Yeah? So what did you hear them say?'

Suddenly she got it. His mimicry. The hard work — how he had become a perfectly assimilated migrant's son. He would beat them at their own game and be Dutcher than the Dutch. Her annoyance was triggered by their similarities: even though they were both born and raised in the Netherlands, not even their fervour and ambition could make them anything more than Moroccans.

'So?' he insisted.

She smiled benignly. 'Fishes. That there was another plate of them coming.'

He threw his arms in the air. 'She's smiling! She can smile!' He hopped to his feet. 'Right away, princess. Fishes. And more vodka. The holiday's not over yet, my friends.'

'To all my friends!' he said a little later, raising his glass. Another borrowed phrase, she figured. He had them for all eventualities. He possessed no firm core, only other people's melodies, to which he danced in step. Her irritation had vanished; now there was only a harmless sort of contempt. She was proud of her own insight into human character.

She could see him on a talk show one day, a day not far from now; a popular guest, with the right commentary for every occasion: an organ-grinder's monkey, drilled in perfect imitation.

Thouraya's was the full, thick laughter of a drunken woman. There was a smudge of lipstick under her bottom lip.

Ilham drank vodka only rarely. The high was pleasant. She viewed things from a distance; Thouraya, willing as could be, Noureddine's composed nonchalance beside her, their preparations. Driss was watching a clip on YouTube and using his free hand to drum out the beat on his thigh. Jalal laid the keycards on the table; he'd succeeded in getting a room for two and a room for four. His scalp was so thin, the bone of his skull almost jabbed its way through, she saw. If she were his mother, she'd feed him till he couldn't eat another bite. The crotch of his trousers hung to just above his knees.

In the not-too-distant future, Noureddine would shake off his friends, she knew; a gentle, gradual break, riverbanks widening and drawing apart. Then his assimilation would be complete.

9

One, two bodies slip through the crack of light. The door clicks shut behind them. Clothes fall to the floor, bodies find the bed, each other. Do they really think she's asleep? They've been drinking hard — they were still at it when she went to bed. Ilham breathes silently. The rustle of sheets, their hands everywhere. She feels their shudders, tastes the honey from their lips, hears the lament that catches in Thouraya's throat as he goes into her. The stab of jealousy. She is ashamed of being awake and ashamed of the shiver of lust and horror.

In Rabat, Thouraya had gone alone with a boy in an opalescent VW with custom hubs and German plates. To a remote spot, close to the grave of a marabou, an ancient shrine with a dilapidated dome. The night was full of sounds. The scream of a jackal, far away. The orange glow above the city in the distance. They had smoked a joint and fucked in the passenger seat.

Slowly, Ilham gets to her feet. She slips out of bed, collects her clothes and shoes by feel, takes her purse from the chair, and leaves the room. For a moment, she thinks they're going to follow her — sorry-sorry-sorry — but nothing happens. She takes the stairs. The hall and lobby are bathed in cold, profuse light. A roll-down shutter has been drawn over the hotel desk. She hesitates before the button that will open the sliding doors — there is no coming back; Thouraya has the keycard. Then she steps out into the warm night.

The neon letters on the roof of the restaurant have been turned off. An occasional car goes ripping down the darkened highway. Where would people be going to at this hour? For what reason? She crosses the car park, throwing a shadow in the light from the hotel spots. Even now, the asphalt is glowing.

There are ten or fifteen cars parked in front of the hotel; theirs is the furthest away. Even at a distance, the smell of decay invades her nostrils. She's never smelled anything worse. She pulls a tissue from her handbag and covers her nose with it. She gags, bile rising in her throat. She opens the door and sits — and then, her head bent to one side, vomits on the asphalt. 'Oh god,' she moans. There has to be a bottle of water in the car somewhere. She can't find it. She pulls the opened carton of Marlboro Lights from under the seat and plucks at the cellophane of a new pack, her fingers trembling. Her throat is dry; the smoke stings but dispels the stench for a bit. She takes a few drags, one after the other, then starts the car.

She drives out of the car park, the windows open. At the roundabout, she doesn't head onto the highway, but takes the turn-off into the countryside. Her vision is blurred; she wipes away the tears that came with the gagging. This smell, she knows, can never be washed away. It will stay with her for a lifetime.

Her gullet is burning. The clock says two twenty-one.

Down a dark country road she drives through the hills, until she sees a turn-off, a path through the gnarled olive trees. She drives slowly, in concentration; the dried soil crunches beneath the tyres. The lights swipe over pale trunks, and she pants in the suffocating stench, an indecent assault. He is not only a stranger now, but an enemy. He has nothing left in common with the nice boy she saw yesterday.

The track winds uphill, the deathly pale xenon lights of the Audi cutting a path in front of her. With a loud bang, a stone ricochets off the chassis.

She stops the car just past a bend and dims the lights.

She climbs out and walks away from the car; beneath the starry sky she is able to start breathing again. Cicadas, and a regular, scraping sound somewhere far away, like a rusty signboard grating in the wind. Misty green starlight floats above the mountain silhouettes.

Beyond those mountains is the sea, which she crossed less than one day ago. That girl there, on deck with her eyes closed and her face to the sun, that's a different person — her life hasn't started yet. In the darkness, her fate is being worked on. A little later it will unfold in its gruesome glory, and it will be as though her whole life was destined to arrive at this; every step she took led to this and not to anything else. If they'd arrived one minute later at that service station outside Tangier, *half* a minute later, they wouldn't have had that accident and they wouldn't have been broke. One little detour on the way to that McDonald's and they would never have met Saleh. If she hadn't said yes that afternoon in Témara, the yes that lay in a nod.

Her life, she thinks, has been one drawn-out choreography, leading, step by step, to his death.

The heat of the night is hardly different from that of the day. It's time. About to touch the boot, her hand falters. She's afraid that he will look up at her with his bloodshot eyes and that his tainted mouth will curse her. Filthy, calumniating words that will turn her life into a hell of pain and loss.

She pulls the suitcases out, tosses them down beside the car. His face has turned dark; in the orange glow of the trunk light she sees that his eyes are sunk far back into the skull, the whites of them wrinkly and dull. She takes a step back and retches. Threads of sour mucus are hanging from her mouth; she feels light in the head. Is she fainting? Don't faint. Not now. Act. She needs to act. She wipes her mouth with her forearm and takes a deep breath.

The warmth of his skin startles her — as warm as though he were still alive. But she had checked again that afternoon — he was dead, dead as can be! She grabs him by one wrist and the other hand and pulls. The body feels like a clump of solid rubber — there's almost no give to it, no matter how she pulls. The edge of the boot is an unassailable hurdle; she lacks the strength to work him over it. One arm is now sticking out of the car; weeping, she tugs at it. 'Come on now,' she begs. 'Please.' She smells shit and rot. His armpit scrapes along the boot's rim. 'Help me now, Murat … Please …' She climbs onto the bumper, grabs him by the belt and leans back, but death has made him leaden and immovable. '*Fuck* you, Murat,' she says through her tears, '*fuck* you.'

His head is hanging over backwards into the cavity for the spare; glistening fluid runs from his mouth into his nose and eyes. Again she curses having been born a girl, weak, helpless; everything people have always told her about women is true. The weaker sex. How could she ever get along without the protection of a man, a father or a husband? Look at the trouble she's in. The stars above her and the chalky white tree trunks all around bear witness to her failure. She is surrounded by the scornful *knowing* of these things.

When she lets go, his body falls back. She slams the boot, washes her sticky hands with dust and wipes them on rough bark until they smart. Then, leaning back against a tree, she smokes. The smoke is hard for her to take, but anything is better than the air of cadaver that has nestled in her airways.

She crushes out the cigarette with the toe of one shoe. Amid the olive trees she turns the car around and drives back down the path. The suitcases she leaves behind.

10

Night had vanished, with the sudden outburst of early-morning light. Roosters in the distance spurred each other on with their cock-a-doodle-doo. Businesspeople left the hotel, pulling their trolley suitcases with one hand, cradling a cup of vending-machine coffee in the other. Ilham sat on the far side of the parking lot, atop a low stone wall that faced the entrance. She was wearing sunglasses, and she said hello to none of the businessmen in return. A sweetish whiff of the oleander blossoms behind her; she was surprised, as though she had expected to never again smell anything other than rotting, rotting.

Were they awake, there in that cool hotel room, their bodies filled with morning lust?

And that hoarse dog up in the hills — what was it

barking at? She sat with her knees pulled up, her arms wrapped around them. The stiffness in her lower back felt better right away. She remained sitting like that, resting her cheek on her arms, until she saw the boys coming out of the sliding doors. They crossed the parking lot, squinting into the morning light. They were having a good time about something; she could hear their laughter as they tossed their luggage into the trunk. Driss saw her as he was climbing in. When he held up his hand, she remained motionless. Now the others saw her too. Noureddine showed no expression at all; he opened the door and disappeared into the back seat. The doors slammed, and Driss and Jalal looked at her as they drove past. Jalal looked longest; he turned all the way around in the passenger seat to look at her, his gaze wide-eyed and questioning.

'Where were you?' Thouraya asked after she opened the door. Ilham shook her head and entered the room without a word. The floor of the little bathroom was wet, the mirror steamed over, wet towels lay in a pile. She undressed and took a long shower.

When she came back into the room, the venetian blinds were open; strips of sunlight gleamed on the carpet. Thouraya was lying on the bed, fully dressed, her finger sliding across the screen of her phone. Ilham dried her hair and twisted the towel into a knot at the top of her head. 'Could I borrow your brush?' she asked. She was about to have her period; she could tell from the tautness in her belly.

'They're gone — you know that, right?' she asked a little later, as she was tying her hair in a ponytail.

Thouraya nodded.

'So,' she asked, 'was it romantic, your little farewell?'

Her friend said nothing.

He took off without saying anything, Ilham thought. She was ready to go, but Thouraya made no move to get up. Ilham asked: 'So why aren't you saying anything?'

'What am I supposed to say?'

'That it didn't completely work out, your little plan.'

'My little plan?' Reluctantly, Thouraya wrested her eyes away from the phone.

'The whole reason to go along with them. You were going to fix it, right?'

'Oh, that.'

'And now they're gone and we still don't have a thing.'

'They paid for the hotel,' Thouraya said breezily. 'And dinner and stuff.'

'Great, that helps a lot.'

'And he left this lying here …' She took a worn wallet from her handbag.

Ilham opened it and pulled out the contents. Bank cards, dirhams, the reassuring euro notes — tens, twenties, even two fifties … But the loveliest of all, the absolute bell-ringer: his credit card.

'Left it *lying here*?' she asked, agog.

'Sort of.'

'Thour, you *rolled* him, really?'

She fell onto the bed, shrieking with laughter. They laughed and laughed, hugged each other and wiped the tears from their eyes.

After a hurried breakfast of tea and croissants from the vending machines, they left the hotel. The hesitation as they approached the car — they took a gulp of air and got in.

Out on the highway, Ilham looked over. Thouraya's hair was blowing wildly in the wind. They smoked one cigarette after the other, in silence. Ilham admired her, her independence and her fearlessness — she took what was coming to her, she was bellicose, in everything, including her desires. Thouraya — and this was what she admired most — had tamed the beast of shame.

From that all the rest had issued forth.

Using Noureddine's Visa card, they filled the tank and bought a bag of bottled water, cookies, chocolate, nuts, and tampons — everything they wanted, and as much as they could carry. Ilham signed for it; his signature was not much more than his name written sloppily.

They passed on the high road above Jaén, sweating out its sins far below. There was no end to the blasted land, the metastases of olive trees along the road. They almost took an exit on a few occasions, but each time there was too much human activity for what they had to do.

Before them now the green flanks of the Sierra Morena, the final range before the Spanish tableland. The road rose gradually. Ilham rummaged through the wallet. The student library card she tossed out the window, along with his ID from the University of Amsterdam. She kept his bank card and credit card; they could use that to get home. The condom in its silver foil packet she waved under her friend's nose. Thouraya's smile in reply was dainty and royal. 'Ooops — just a little too late,' she said.

The condom flew out the window, followed by the wallet, empty now except for a few photos of Noureddine with different girls, taken in train-station photo booths. Why wasn't she surprised to see that the girls were blondes? 'Bye-bye, Noureddine,' she said quietly, then glanced in the mirror to see if the wallet was still in sight on the asphalt.

Every once in a while, when they went through a curve or changed lanes, the current of air passing through the car shifted and the toxic stench took their breath away; their nausea was hard and fierce.

Through the mountains they slipped out onto the *meseta*. There were rolling fields with horses, and watercolour hills on the horizon. The faint yellow monochromes of grain fields beneath the pounding sun. They passed brand-new service stations and public facilities, rectangular and spotless, where the loneliness of the scale-model reigned supreme. The first humans had yet to enter them.

Ilham stared at the pink dust devils above the plain, wobbly columns drifting slowly across the earth. Far away, so far that the eye could barely get a purchase on them, were huge bales of straw piled into a high wall; their contours crumbled in the light. Further away on the plateau the earth was red and cracked; rain evaporated before it could strike the ground; a mineral mist rendered the soil brackish. Once, this land had been wooded and fertile, and in the summer the herds descended from the hills to this plain, but a steady process of land degradation had turned large tracts of it into a steppe of esparto grass and sand. The water table sank year after year; someday all would be desert here; tendrils of sand were already creeping across the road. Man and beast withdrew from the exhausted soil; sand and dust were blown across the flats. What remained was arid growth on the stony, blown-out ground. Farmers cursed the soil and abandoned their farms and villages.

The space around her made Ilham dizzy, vertigo on a horizontal plane; yes, here in this desolation was where it had to happen. The asphalt in front of them dissolved in silvery vibrations; the earth blanched to a chalky white, as though a thermal blast had laid it all to ash.

Just past noon Thouraya took an exit and drove towards a village, heralded in the distance by a tall grain silo. They drove slowly through the streets. Nowhere a sign of life: the streets were empty, the shutters drawn tight. The people, if there were any still around, had withdrawn behind thick, cool walls. Leaflets under the wipers of parked cars flapped feebly in the scorching wind.

As they drove out of the village, they passed, as though by a miracle, two girls, still young, wearing shorts and flip-flops. Were they the ones who had put the leaflets on those cars? They slipped past the girls, as though in slow motion, and underwent their lethargic glance, the faint spark of curiosity, like that of a horse at pasture.

Once they had passed the final house, Ilham saw a town sign reading 'Turleque'. They switched off the sound on the navigation system, the voice that was trying to take them back to the highway.

Leaving the asphalt, they made a few lefts and rights on unpaved roads that ran between the fields. Whirlwinds drifted across the plain, faraway and close by. They were alone on an endlessly flat surface, not a car or tractor to be seen. A cloud of dust rose up behind them from the metalled road, and was blown away. The grain silo had disappeared from sight.

Across the crumbly earth they drove on, to where they thought no one would see them. Ilham was amazed at the occasional holm oak she saw, the perfect circle of shadow at its foot; the trees were stunted and wore a dark-green crown atop their low grey trunks. This was how a child drew a tree. How did they survive here? How could anything survive here?

There were traces of human construction,

abandoned wells and outbuildings of clay and stone surrounded by a few trees. Straight above all these things smouldered the big sun; the earth could burst into flame at any moment.

A sand spout came towards them from the left, across a fallow, ruby-red plot of ground — Ilham saw the seething funnel at its foot and how the plume fanned out and grew weaker as it rose.

Straight in front of them was another, pale and furious, the colour of the road itself. Thouraya slowed to avoid it and forgot about the whirlwind to their left — suddenly they found themselves caught in a vicious rattle of grit, chaff, and prickles. Blinded, Thouraya hit the brakes, and the sand spout came straight through the open windows; they could no longer see a thing, and they screamed. The noise was deafening, then it was over. The car had come to a halt, pitched across the road. The unearthly rattle moved on. The wipers swept the dust from the windshield.

On the far side of the dirt road, above the field of grain, the whirlwind changed colour and pursued its wild dance in bright yellow.

The dashboard, the seats, the two of them — everything was covered with a confetti of dust, bits of chaff and thistles. They wiped their faces and shook the debris from their hair.

–

A little further along they left the dirt track and drove across a field of grain that had already been gathered, towards a ruined outbuilding of clay. Its walls were eroded, melted more like; beams stuck out of it like ribs from a carcass. They passed it and drove further across the field, until the dirt track was so far behind them that they could no longer see it. When they stepped out of the car, stubble crackled beneath their feet.

Ilham walked a little way into the field. Above her head, the swifts were crying their *sri, sri*. She stared at the horizon — it wasn't a matter of her taking in the space around her, the space was taking *her* in. It was as though she had landed outside the limits of her body and was being scattered across the plain. The only thing she heard was the quiet rush of the wind and a single fly, a frantic, starved fly revived by the nearby smell of death. Through her lashes she looked at a snowy white cloud, the only one in the sky, which was otherwise as empty as the earth below.

Thouraya was picking burrs from her clothes, a cigarette in the corner of her mouth and one eye squeezed shut against the smoke.

Ilham walked back to the car.

Her friend handed her a cigarette. They nodded to

each other, braced themselves and took a deep breath.

The trunk popped open. Blowing smoke from their nostrils, they bent over the dead boy. The thick, syrupy smell of corpse rose up to meet them. The blood in his eyes had turned black, the eyes themselves had a murky film across them. Ilham heard a deep groan beside her. His skin was wet and marbled; it looked like he was sweating heavily. They both seized him by a trouser leg and pulled his legs outside the car. The rigor mortis was gone; he felt only soft and sickening.

Thouraya dropped the leg, leaned over, and vomited as she stumbled away from the car. Ilham did the same, almost immediately. The one prompted the other: as soon as one of them started vomiting, the other followed suit immediately.

Ilham was sweating all over. She wiped the tears from her eyes and helped her friend to her feet.

They pulled in unison now, first on his trousers, then by his belt, and finally by his t-shirt until they had him out of the trunk. The body fell limply to the ground. A colourless discharge trickled from his nose and mouth; his trousers were soaked with his own excrement.

They moved away from the car, snorting, gasping for air.

'Oh my god,' Thouraya said at last. She couldn't take her eyes off the body on the ground.

Ilham fetched a bottle from the car and poured water over her friend's shaking hands. 'We did it,' Thouraya said as she rinsed her hands. 'We *fucking* did it …'

Ilham nodded, a feeble smile playing at her lips. She sank to her knees and rubbed her hands in the dust. Thouraya held the bottle for her. A thin stream of water fell onto the earth, a dark spot in the dust between the stubble, and evaporated fast.

Thouraya brushed her hair back with her fingers and walked to the car, giving the body a wide berth. She pulled the Audi away from him, the trunk still open. 'Come on, let's get out of here,' she shouted.

Ilham nodded. She looked again at the paltry pile of limbs and textile, then walked towards the car, in lonely silhouette between heaven and earth.

'Shouldn't we say something?'

'Like what?'

'A prayer or something?'

'You know one?'

'No.'

'Me neither. Come on, move.'

Ilham took Murat's plastic bag from the trunk and shook it out on the ground. A comb, some underwear, a disposable razor, and a little leather pouch, tied tightly with string. She picked it up and felt it. Soft, it gave way to her touch. Holding the marabou's bundle, she walked over to him. She knelt and laid it in his open hand. Metallic green flies were crawling over his body — god knows where they all came from so suddenly. She heard the feverish, aggressive zooming, a noise so isolated and intense against the hissing silence that it sounded as though they were scurrying over her eardrums.

'Sorry,' she said, and stood up.

At the car she turned around again. '*Beslama*, Murat,' she murmured, then climbed in quickly. The plastic bag wafted up and blew into the fields. Thouraya touched the gas, and the car leapt forward. Ilham looked back. Through the veil of dust she saw him disappear quickly, nothing other than a blackened trunk or a windswept piece of plastic sheeting on the immeasurable plain.